Inspiring | Educating | Creating | Entertaining

Brimming with creative inspiration, how-to projects, and useful information to enrich your everyday life, quarto.com is a favourite destination for those pursuing their interests and passions.

Published by arrangement with Debbie Bibo Agency

First published in 2023 by Frances Lincoln Children's Books,
an imprint of The Quarto Group.
1 Triptych Place,
London, SE1 9SH
T (0)20 7700 6700 F (0)20 7700 8066
www.Quarto.com

ISBN 978-0-7112-8333-6
eISBN 978-0-7112-8335-0

The illustrations were created with gouache
Set in Futura

Published by Peter Marley
Edited by Lucy Brownridge
Designed by Holly Jolley and Marianna Coppo
Translated by Debbie Bibo
Production by Dawn Cameron

Printed in Guangdong, China TT022023

1 3 5 7 9 8 6 4 2

the best bad day ever

Marianna Coppo

I can tell from the minute I wake up
that it is going to be a bad day.

First of all, it's cloudy.

There aren't enough
chocolate chips in my cookies.

And my glass of milk
is half empty.

The water is ice-cold.

And the toothpathte tinglethes my thongue.

Even Pepito is in a bad mood today.

Outside everyone is happy.

BEEEP!

Lucky them.

I arrive late to school,
but it's not a big deal.

I don't feel like doing
anything anyway.

APPLE

TREE

Even when I try to do something,

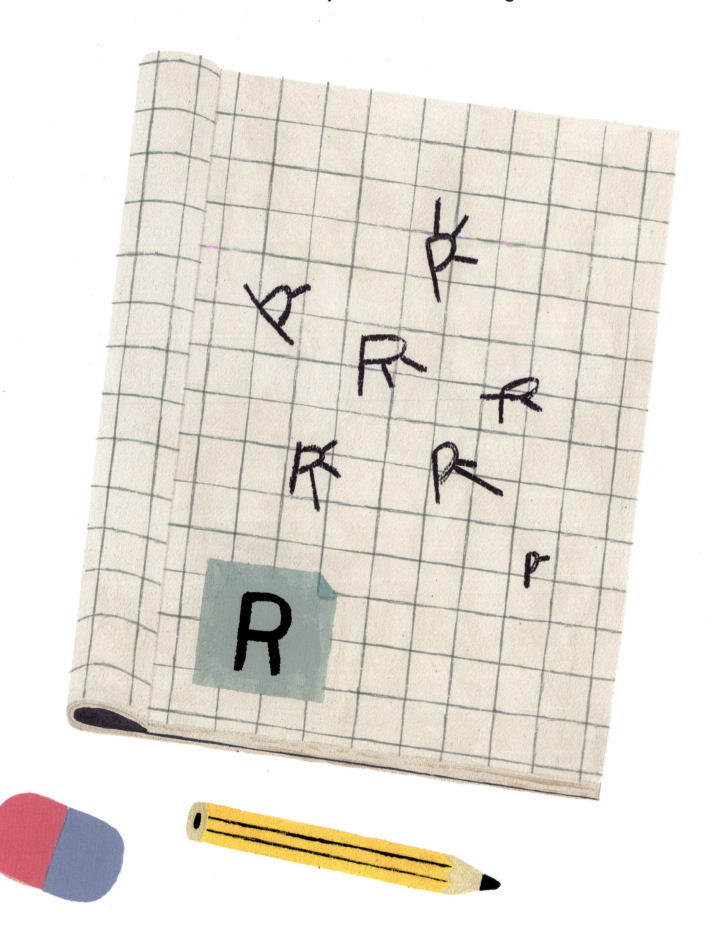

nothing comes out right.

At circle time,

The cat says
"MEOW."

The chick says
"PEEP PEEP."

the frog says
"RIBBIT."

The pig says
"OINK."

Pepito says
nothing.

I say
"HRUMPH."

No one understands me.

1 2 3

At playtime,
we play hide-and-seek.

I don't know how,
but they find us immediately.

At snack time, I get a pear.
I do not like pears.

But I love apples.

At nap time,
everyone is asleep.

Except for us.

Together, the afternoon
goes by too quickly.

And the bell rings too soon.

"How was your day?"

"It was the BEST BAD DAY EVER!"

Wow!

It looks like
it's going to be
a beautiful day.